Cow's Big Kick

by A.H. Benjamin

Illustrated by Rupert Van Wyk

W

FRANKLIN WATTS

LONDON•SYDNEY

First published in 2009 by
Franklin Watts
338 Euston Road
London
NW1 3BH

Franklin Watts Australia
Level 17/207 Kent Street
Sydney
NSW 2000

Text © A.H. Benjamin 2009
Illustration © Rupert Van Wyk 2009

A CIP catalogue record for this book is available
from the British Library.

ISBN 978 0 7496 8514 0 (hbk)
ISBN 978 0 7496 8520 1 (pbk)

Series Editor: Jackie Hamley
Editor: Melanie Palmer
Series Advisor: Dr Hilary Minns
Series Designer: Peter Scoulding

Printed in China

Franklin Watts is a division of
Hachette Children's Books,
an Hachette UK company.
www.hachette.co.uk

For Nassera and Mike
– A.H. Benjamin.

Cow was always kicking things by mistake.

Cow kicked over
a watering can.

"Watch out!" said Cat.

Then Cow kicked
a flowerpot.

"Be careful!" said Dog.

Cow kicked an apple.

"Ouch!" said Horse.

Cow kicked the washing basket.

"What a mess!" said the farmer's wife.

Everyone was fed up with Cow kicking things.

"I know what Cow needs!" said the farmer.

Cow kicked the ball ...

"Goal!" everyone
shouted.

Puzzle Time!

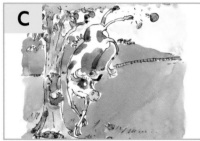

Put these pictures in the right order and retell the story!

clumsy

smart

clever

messy

Which words describe Cow and which describe the farmer?

Turn over for answers!

Notes for adults

TADPOLES are structured to provide support for newly independent readers. The stories may also be used by adults for sharing with young children.

Starting to read alone can be daunting. **TADPOLES** help by providing visual support and repeating words and phrases. These books will both develop confidence and encourage reading and rereading for pleasure.

If you are reading this book with a child, here are a few suggestions:

1. Make reading fun! Choose a time to read when you and the child are relaxed and have time to share the story.
2. Talk about the story before you start reading. Look at the cover and the blurb. What might the story be about? Why might the child like it?
3. Encourage the child to retell the story, using the jumbled picture puzzle as a starting point. Extend vocabulary with the matching words to characters puzzle.
4. Discuss the story and see if the child can relate it to their own experience.
5. Give praise! Remember that small mistakes need not always be corrected.

Answers

Here is the correct order:

1.c 2.b 3.f 4.e 5.a 6.d

Words to describe Cow:
clumsy, messy

Words to describe the farmer:
clever, smart

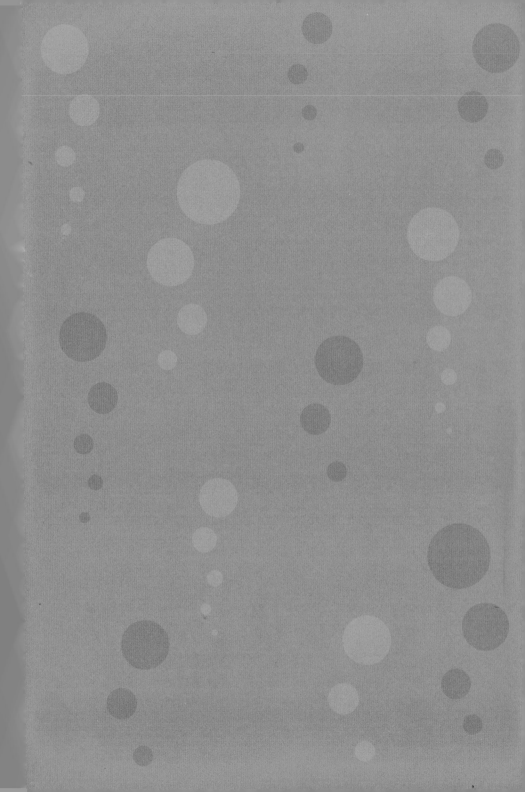